SCIENCE KIDS
Colors

GREEN

Jared Siemens

LET'S READ

AV²

BY WEIGL™

ADDED VALUE • AUDIO VISUAL

Go to www.av2books.com, and enter this book's unique code.

BOOK CODE

N 284020

AV² by Weigl brings you media enhanced books that support active learning.

AV² provides enriched content that supplements and complements this book. Weigl's AV² books strive to create inspired learning and engage young minds in a total learning experience.

Your AV² Media Enhanced books come alive with...

Audio
Listen to sections of the book read aloud.

Video
Watch informative video clips.

Embedded Weblinks
Gain additional information for research.

Try This!
Complete activities and hands-on experiments.

Key Words
Study vocabulary, and complete a matching word activity.

Quizzes
Test your knowledge.

Slide Show
View images and captions, and prepare a presentation.

... and much, much more!

Published by AV² by Weigl
350 5th Avenue, 59th Floor New York, NY 10118
Websites: www.av2books.com   www.weigl.com

Library of Congress Control Number: 2014934864

ISBN 978-1-4896-1250-2 (hardcover)
ISBN 978-1-4896-1251-9 (softcover)
ISBN 978-1-4896-1252-6 (single user eBook)
ISBN 978-1-4896-1253-3 (multi-user eBook)

Printed in the United States of America in North Mankato, Minnesota
1 2 3 4 5 6 7 8 9 0 18 17 16 15 14

042014
WEP150314

3 4873 00506 4340

Project Coordinator: Aaron Carr
Designer: Mandy Christiansen

Weigl acknowledges Getty Images and iStock as the primary image suppliers for this title.

SCIENCE KIDS
Colors
GREEN

CONTENTS

What is this color?
I have seen it before!

4

It is green things I see!
Will you help me find more?

I see green
on each stair.

I see green
on this chair.

Is there green in your home?
Can you tell me where?

7

Green is the color of food people eat.

Can you think of any green foods that are sweet?

I see
a green block.

I see
a green ball.

Which is your most favorite green toy of all?

**Look down
at the ground.**

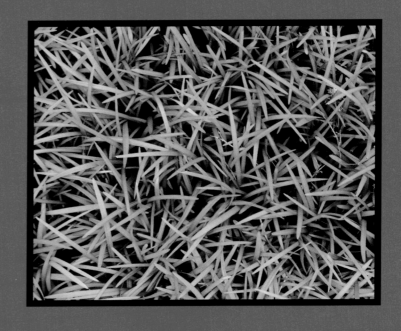

**Look up
in the trees.**

I see green leaves and grass that move in the breeze.

I see
a green bird.

I see
a green snake.

How many green animals
can you find near a lake?

Playgrounds are fun.
There are fun things to do.

You could swing on green bars and ride a slide, too!

I see
a green pencil.

I see
a green book.

18

Is there green at your school?
Please help me look.

Green can mean go.

Green can mean grow.

**Green can mean other things.
How many do you know?**

BIKE ROUTE

Find where these green things belong in this book.

22

Go back through the pages and have a close look!

KEY WORDS

Research has shown that as much as 65 percent of all written material published in English is made up of 300 words. These 300 words cannot be taught using pictures or learned by sounding them out. They must be recognized by sight. This book contains 64 common sight words to help young readers improve their reading fluency and comprehension. This book also teaches young readers several important content words, such as proper nouns. These words are paired with pictures to aid in learning and improve understanding.

Page	Sight Words First Appearance
4	before, have, I, is, it, this, what
5	find, help, me, more, see, things, will, you
6	on
7	can, home, in, tell, there, where, your
8	eat, food, of, people, the
9	any, are, that, think
10	a
11	all, most, which
12	at, down, look, trees, up
13	and, leaves, move
15	animals, how, many, near
16	do, to
17	could, too
18	book
19	school
20	go, grow, mean
21	know, other
22	these
23	back, close, pages, through

Page	Content Words First Appearance
4	color
5	green
6	chair, stair
10	ball, block
11	toy
12	ground
13	breeze, grass
14	bird, snake
15	lake
16	playgrounds
17	bars, slide
18	pencil

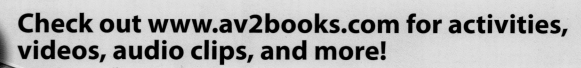